DARK AT NOON

Collection of Short Stories by

John Barroso

Translated from Portuguese by

Linda Loewer

I0686901

Stories originally appeared in
Portuguese in *Contos Psicológicos*
(Raquinho and Insult) and *Almas
Invisíveis* (Malhada and Araçatuba,
Little Party, Cunning Adam, The Dog).

Four stories are new (The Right Hand,
Chaw, Glass of Wine, and Brief
History of the Kingdom of Oranoslob),
not published in Portuguese.

Notes from the author:

I am indebted to Linda Loewer for translating these stories.

As influence on my writings, I am indebted to the writings of Raymond Carver, Mary Robison, Ann Beattie, Amy Hampel, Tobias Wolf, K. J. Stevens, Frederick Barthelme, Bobbie N. Mason, Ernest Hemingway, Graciliano Ramos, and very importantly, Dalton Trevisan.

I am also indebted to Professor Maria Ivonette S. Silva, from the Federal University of Uberlândia, for bringing my writings to the attention of Ph.D. students in Literature.

To the readers, I can only assure an encounter with the brutal realism of realization, besides engaging reading dominated by crafted writing. In Minimalism, writing a carefully conceived picture that is real enough to shock and horrific enough to enchant the thinking minds. I am a writer who does not write to pass time. I have a message to pass on, in a very specific way, about very specific things. I will require the readers to think along, and to feel along.

*Drawings by John Barroso.

Stories order:

Malhada and Araçatuba

The old man ruled. He looked over his glasses and ordered: "separate the cows". It was like that: few words, much action and everyone feared him. Malhada had been the children´s favorite cow, on her they leaned, they milked her, they rode her, the pulled her ears, they walked underneath her and Malhada not even moved. She knew how to love and be loved. The other was Araçatuba, which on the first off springs gave three buckets of milk but after nine off springs, it fell to two liters. Her day has come.

We ate in silence, broken by sporadic comments of politics or useful things. The old did not talk trivial, but he liked to insinuate, to laugh after suggesting an idea that left the listener mentally confused, to soon realize that the old man was truly a sarcastic thinker. Always, it was his habit to drink a pinga before the meals to warm the throat, but at work he was rude, he fired the cowhands without thought or blinking, at the slightest disobedience. We ate thinking about the next topic. The old man did not like thoughtless conversations. There was always this tension in what to say. The women groveled for him; the men conceded him quiet obedience. He paid on time, and on Friday afternoons he gave everyone pinga while he himself drank some, and for a few minutes he was conveniently loved. There was always one hour of happiness on Fridays. And we ate rice, beans and steak while the sounds of mooing and grazing cattle filled the long silences. The cows had been separated. It was me who asked to see.

We ate that typical steak, with bright white rice and beans with nothing, other than salt and oil. Chickens cackled every second. The ducks paraded, lined up, filling the yard with droppings, even so we still ate those delicious beans with rare sirloin in deep thoughts, filtering what to say. "The price of coffee rose", said the old man, suggesting that I commented. "It rose, it must be good to sell everything quickly", "It is", he responded. If anyone disagreed, he would come out of his shell and destroy whoever he was, but I always commented without creating conflicts. The old woman, wife to the old man, passed, putting more steaks on the plate, more beans. Always quiet, for she knew nothing about business, her role was to serve with harmony, but also to agree by nodding. We all ate quietly, waiting for the old man open a new topic.

From far off we saw the cowhand coming, walking like a cowhand, swaying his arms, hat lowered in the front, always inspecting things to find something to fix, chewing hay. To the cowhands, to be always alert meant the guarantee of work and protection of the old man. "He is a good cowhand", he would say, about those that were alert, who found things to fix.

"Morning" and we responded "morning". "Do you want to eat? Sit there", said the old man. The offer was mandatory politeness and the answer, as well. Although hungry "No, thanks", replied the cowhand and went straight to the subject: "Corintiana will calve". The old man would always look over his glasses and the cowhand to the ground and responded in short sentences: "put her in the paddock". The cowhand already knew this but had to receive the order, in submission, as if they were incapable of deciding. The cowhands came almost in a line, each one always had two topics: "and the black horse is limping". And the old man taught him: "See if it has a nail in the hoofs". The mornings ran like this and so cowhands and boss, all exercised their roles. After their questions and orders received, the cowhands slowly walked afar, to the corral, to the corn hut, to wherever awaited the next chore. It was always like this, as if at lunch time the old man dispatched, like accountants do, and the cowhands came in submission to announce daily events, awaiting obvious orders and the old man deciding what was already known. His decision was at the same time an order and a formality.

On that day, finally, there came that certain cowhand, who would take me to the slaughterhouse. "There comes Léo". I then saw the man, thin like everyone, tall, kind of pale, arriving with confident air. "Morning". "Morning", we said at the same time. Soon, the old man, happily said "This is the man who wants to see the cows die". And the cowhand responded, "you will see everything". And me, there, got a bit frightened. It was me who asked to see the cowhand kill a cow. It seems that every man always see those things to be macho. I asked, and now the two cows are already in the corral, waiting without knowing. "You will see the two", said the cowhand, timidly, not knowing who I was. In shining shoes, I could be an important person. The old man was the architect of everything: he gave the cowhand and gave the cows to grant my request. "Thank you", I said and he moved his head, one time only, very slowly downwards, one time only and in slow movement, indicating the discrete macho manner with which cowhands say "you're welcome". "Some pinga?", asked the old man and the cowhand said "no, I've had lunch". Everyone there drank a shot before lunch to warm their throat. It is a typical paulista thing, even the children, those that reached fifteen, or are at least as tall as a man, except the girls, drink to warm their throat. The girls are not permitted to drink, pinga is macho thing, the girls stay inside, sometimes discretely looking from the windows, they never walk near men, so as not to distract them or generate harmful comments of the girls. The girls are always well protected from anything bad, preserved from any unnecessary exposures to men so that they don't become defamed, so they are worth more at marriage. These were orders from the old man. The old woman comes with more food, serves quietly, sits quietly and seems to like her role of agreeing by nodding. She participates in everything.

The cowhand sat quietly and we took the last bites. He looked at his hand or at his boots, which looked like cheap boots. There nobody worked in sandals or shorts. The cowhands knew to obey and always looked to the ground as if looking for the presence of seeds or weed. The old man looked straight ahead and when he gave orders there were few words but unmistakable. Always, after that lunch with salt and steak flavor, a small and sweet and strong coffee. "Coffee?". Léo rose without a word, rubbing his rough hands, creating a grating sound. Refusing the coffee would be an unforgiving insult. We drank from the little espresso coffee cups in small gulps, for the old woman, ready and servile, gave us hot and sweet coffee. Within minutes, the old man arose and walked to the pickup truck and me and the cowhand got in the Beatle and there we went, one to kill and the other to see the deaths.

The corral was big, with one covered part with concrete floor, still covered with cow manure, almost dry. The other part was of dirt floor, with manure still wet from the light rain that fell in the morning. There was a section of the corral that had a tight, long chute with a gate at the end. The two cows were on the uncovered part, and the cowhand, ready to show his abilities, had sharpened the knives hours before. The other cowhands would say "morning" and I would respond, and they would ask "all good?". There no one introduce themselves or said, "my pleasure", which is a gay thing, according to them. Everyone talked excitedly and walked with the confidence of machos. "Good", I responded. They didn´t ask who I was but I might be an important person, wearing shoes in the corral, wanting to see a cow die, a city people thing, wanting to be man like them. Soon they started talking about thousand things, from cows to horses to cars to fences. They talked about useful things, for talking about women was prohibited, especially when a stranger was nearby. He could tell the old man. The cowhand, with knives in hand, ordered the first cow to enter, a thing that the other cowhands quickly did, and Malhada came walking quickly, still chewing the last supper, into the walled chute, perhaps thinking about running quickly to the other side, like she did many times when they gave her a vaccine. But Léo closed the gate in her face, and a third cowhand put a beam across, behind the cow, kind of squeezing her and she tried to jump but was already confined. Léo gently put a lasso on her neck and carefully passed a rope underneath the wood board, raising the other end, which he tied to a post. Malhada stayed calm, chewing and waiting perhaps a child sit on her back as they always did. One of the cowhands, sitting high one chute, spoke of something he saw on tv the night before. The cow snorted and tried to wiggle, but Léo, interrupting his talk about the corn planting he would do, slowly ran his thumb on the cows head, looking for a low central point and the cow snorted, and Leo calmly inserted a long knife, very thin, that went in slowly and firmly through that low point and Leo continued to push the knife, slowly but firmly and the cow snorted and bellowed loudly, and when I looked the cow rolled her eyes with the white to the outside and her tongue dropped out more than ten inches and blood dripped, running down her face, running down quickly, dripping all over her face, running passed her nose, and Malhada grunted a lot and bellowed deep, without breathing. It was a lot of hot air coming out of her lungs. Leo then said "germinated seeds, guys", referring to his corn plantation, while now he stabbed the second knife, this much larger and also long, and at this moment the cow fell onto her front knees, her back legs still standing and Leo then inserted the thin, long knife underneath to reach the heart and a lot of blood gushed from her chest and the cow still made a sound of wind and fell and Leo then inserted the knife again, about five inches to the side of the first point, and the cow, fallen and bloody, trembled, but no longer snorted. "Monsanto", said Leo about the corn seeds and the other cowhand said, "good production" and they talked about these things. I looked at the cow, that no longer made any sounds, but clearly trembled around the neck and talk continued. Even Leo´s boots got a bit of blood, something he did not even notice. Engaged in the animated conversation, they did not realize Malhada no longer moved, her tongue sticking out, head laying in her own blood, eyes rolled back in her head, white. Quiet, as always, she knew how love and be loved.

On the uncovered part of the corral, the other cow, Araçatuba, desperately dug a whole from under the gate, trying to escape, seemingly predicting her future. She beat her hoofs on the group, making a little hole before she was lassoed by skillful Leo, who swung the lasso in the air and threw it right around her head, a throw so perfect, and purposeful that one of the cowhands screamed "this guy is good". Araçatuba, on the lasso, grunted a lot, stalled a lot and was pulled by force into the chute, grunting and blocked from behind with a beam. She grunted, desperately, and tried to move, jump. She was a good milk cow, but now she only gave two quarts. And Leo, with perfection, one more time sinking that thin and long knife into Araçatuba's nape, who now started to grunt deeply, creating a sound of deep breath, loud and trembling and the blood flowing into the air almost hit Leo´s face, who skillfully moved to the side with precision. She was a good milk cow but now she is worth nothing. Her eyes turned into her head and an enormous tongue hung down dripping a thick drool and her grunting was now deep and long, quite different from her mooing when the milkman called her by name "Araçatuba, Araçatuba, Araçatuba", and she mooed to her baby every morning before they milked her. Now she grunted low, slow, continued. Her breath was one of tiredness, more air coming out than going in, her body fell over her legs and Leo stabbed her on the heart and said he had to go to town later buy vaccine. Araçatuba trembled a bit and suddenly, stopped moving, stopped breathing, her eyes though continued turned inside her head, white, and the cowhands started preparing to leave for the next chore. Leo stomped his boots hard on the ground to free it of blood, adjusted his belt and came down from the improvised steps, while Araçatuba stayed there, laying, kind of twisted, with her big tits of a gyr cow to the sides, some white drops of milk ran down the board, mixing with her blood. The cowhands rolled the lasso, opened the gate and Leo held the two knives, still red and I followed him, quietly thinking of Malhada and Araçatuba.

In the absence of Leo, the other cowhands seemed to speak more. Three cowhands dragged Araçatuba on top of the cement base to cut her off, already talking about sirloin and culotte steaks. Leo walked to the well where there was a bucket with water, already awaiting, and washed his hands and the knives, throwing some water on the bloody boots. "Are you thinking about buying a butcher shop?", he asked, probing. "No, I just wanted to see". "Good then", he answered, not knowing well who I was. Raising his hands high, he reached a bottle and a shot cup that were hiding under the clay roof tiles, "Do you want some pinga?", "Yes, I do", and both of us gave a small smile and drank in quick gulps without face motion upon swallowing. It went down burning and I asked, "how many acres is your corn?" and he said "ten, all flat", and slapped me on the shoulder in a gesture of friendship, already walking to his Beatle. I walked with him, stepping on cow's dung without caring about it, thinking about the stressless life of these cowhands, and trying to talk about corn and plantations. This Leo is really a good person, calm, gentle, and self-controlled. After a short trip, I got out, I thanked and he, very politely made himself available. Before I shut the door, he reminded me with airs of friendship that at the end of the day we would eat that soft meat with fresh fried cassava. It would be a happy dinner, served with pinga, sirloin and culotte, with animated talks and the typical, gentle harmony that abounds on the farms.

Raquinho

Our fun that week was terrorizing Raquinho. It was my best friend's idea. He was always having ideas and, I don't know why, I always helped him put them into action.

Raquinho was thirteen years old too but he looked like a kid of ten, from hunger. It was also from hunger that he had a giant belly where roundworms had set up quarters. His head looked huge because of his skinny body. Our practice of terrorizing him consisted of chasing him at high speed, something that was easy given how weak he was. So we would run alongside him, neck and neck, to confuse the School Monitor. Rape.

Terrified, Raquinho's eyes bulged out, his thoughts imagining the pain, apparent on his starving face. My best friend described the final moment in graphic detail and then reveled in Raquinho's look of sheer horror. Standing in line to go back to the classroom, my best friend ogled Raquinho's butt with exaggerated theatrics. The poor kid could sense the desire of eager eyes pressing into his behind, betrayed by two quivering lines sliding down to his chin. A paralyzed Raquinho stared straight ahead, as if he had already given in to his fate. My best friend really knew how to get under someone's skin.

Raquinho ran almost slowly, his hungry body bumping into ours, heightening his distress as he felt the strength of our bodies upon impact. The feel of our muscles accentuated his smallness. His silence was no doubt ripe with expectant thoughts of our hands holding him hard from behind. When we collided, he recoiled in a gesture of submission, letting us dominate him, which left us incredibly euphoric.

It would be Friday. "He'll keep thinking about it and counting the hours," my best friend said, laughing loudly as he anticipated the damages of the scheduled date. Come Friday, Raquinho had already run a few kilometers. To tell the truth, he wasn't running by then; he was walking, slowed down by the roundworms, and also to save his energy for the moment of submission. Perhaps he'd thought about this moment and decided to deal with the pain, as long as no one saw. He'd never complained to the School Monitor, or said anything to the principal, his teacher, or his mother. He just ran in a kind of quick walk, without blinking, expressionless, like he was a dead kid walking fast.

At the end of every recess, my best friend and I, sweated up either from playing soccer or from running after Raquinho, would go to the restroom to wash our hands and laugh out loud at that poor soul whose existence was about making us happy. We'd laugh, imitate his slow little run, my best friend talking about his malnourished butt and how his small, thin eyes despaired, looking inward. And he'd give a contented laugh.

Friday arrived and we decided to toy with our victim for another week to aggravate his suffering. That Friday we came up alongside him, threw our heavy bodies on him, and my best friend described the merciless penetration to him, finishing off by advising him of its painful postponement. His slow little run, his failure to shout out or tell on us, it all seemed to invite us to press him even harder. My best friend began to suspect that Raquinho liked it, that he actually wanted it. "Don't worry. He's going to whimper," and he'd break into loud guffaws again, a contagious laughter that always had me joining in.

Night fell and I went out for a spin on the Schwinn ten-speed I'd gotten for Christmas the year before. As I came around a corner, there was Raquinho lying in the light of a streetlamp, trying to get up off the ground. He was being beaten by his mother with a wooden stick. His mouth was bleeding and his head too. Even in the vague glow of night under the streetlamp, you could see that his arms, legs, nose, and eyes were all bloody, and the ground as well.

His mother was hitting him with the stick on his mouth, head, ears. Each blow made a dull thud, accompanied by a swallowed moan. Neither Raquinho nor his mother said anything. It was like mute theater, each one playing a role. There was blood all over the place. When his mother saw me, she didn't care much and kept on hitting him for another minute or two. Raquinho moved slowly, groaned like crazy, and his mother struck hard, as if she were killing a bug on the ground.

My right foot on the pedal, I stood there watching, paralyzed. There was Raquinho, bloodied and beaten up but not even crying. Not a word, not a scream. Shaking, I swung my bike around and rushed away, almost fleeing. The sounds of the stick and the smothered moans matched the repeated movements of the woman's silhouette. Raquinho didn't scream, didn't say a thing. It was like he was a dead man taking a beating.

In the classroom on Monday, there was Raquinho. The teacher looked at him without so much as a blink and proceeded with the class on intransitive verbs. The Monitor took a long look at the black-and-blue marks on Raquinho's rachitic face and signaled with his whistle, "Let's wash our hands after the second bell." When Raquinho saw me, he remembered the wheels on my bicycle, the gleam of the handlebars farther up, my tall body, head high, watching behind his mother on the night of the beating. He looked down at the ground in shame and stepped quietly in line.

Meanwhile, my best friend had hit me on the back, all set to run after Raquinho. I hesitated, and he said, "Let's go!" But I didn't. I pretended I wanted to go to the bathroom and started walking off the other way. After insisting a bit, my best friend roared with laughter, this time laughing at me and asking if I was turning chicken. "I'm tired." Alone, he gave up having his fun with Raquinho, at least for a day. Weakened and marked, Raquinho had a day off; he didn't need to run that Monday.

In the days that followed, my best friend didn't invite me to run after Raquinho anymore. He got himself another best friend, and they started running after other weaklings. There were always a few scrawny fellows who scared easy. I didn't tell anybody about the scene under the streetlamp, but once in a while the thought of it troubled me. One day I ran into Raquinho's mother at the grocery store. She looked at me and seemed to recognize me. I shuddered and turned away, pretending not to know her. The boy didn't look at all like his mother; maybe he'd been adopted.

At school, I knew it all; I was always one of the best students. Raquinho was stupid and never knew anything; he had a big head but he was stupid. He was starving too; in less than a minute he'd down the pink milk handed out by the school at recess. He'd tip his head back, swallowing like an animal sucking air from the box. One day the teacher asked me to sit with Raquinho and teach him some grammar rules. My best friend looked at me and gave a snicker. "An intransitive verb, Raquinho, doesn't need a complement to form the predicate." Raquinho looked at me frightened, either because I was there or because of the complicated words. There were his terrified eyes again, but he didn't say anything. He stared dead ahead at the notebook. The teacher, so beautiful, looked at me with guile and smiled discreetly. Far away, at the other edge of the classroom, my best friend watched and laughed; he roared with laughter and contempt, pointing at me as if I were a weakling.

Cunning Adam

Adam was big to play in the street but he pushed tires and we pushed metal hoop with a long stick. We ran on the soft sand on Rua do Sapo street in August when the water truck drove along spraying water to tamp the dust that the women always complained about. So, Rua do Sapo gained an air of sophistication, without dust at least at dusk, when we ran and screamed, and the women made rice and beans that smelt so good that it awakened our hunger. It was a street without lights, without water or sewer and many pieces of plastic and glass mixed with the sand. The yards had many plants and small trees where we ran to quickly pee or the other. Thus, the yards were also contaminated, a thing the mothers gave the kids the cleaning of the yards as chores or punishment. We ran barefoot. The only car in the street was the city ambulance because the driver lived there. Girls younger than ten sometimes played with us but the older ones were kept in by the parents. It was said that girls older than ten were a headache, but the little ones also liked to burn plastic on the end of stick, in the dark to see spinning lines of colorful fire.

But that night was special, because I saw the legs and the naked behind of a woman for the first time and for the first time it gave a stirring. "Are you horny, dummy?" said Adam, laughing. It was about ten at night, just about time to go in, soon the mothers would call, but that night the two sides of the street were quiet, listening. We even stopped running, playing tag, the pushing of wheels, we sat in the dark of a small tree. Adam was the oldest and he said interesting things like "what a hottie". We wanted to be like him, to say things, but we did not know how. With him we lost our shame and became more grown up. We learned with him. That night of screams and sounds, after she passed by us running, he taught us, without realizing, how to jerk off just by doing the motions. We were a bunch of ten-year-old kids, Adam was sixteen. When she ran he saw her beautiful legs from afar and said "look there, what a hottie, what legs". And the woman, without seen us, passed right by our side, walking, almost running, looking back. When she passed, Adam whispered "what an ass" and we looked, intrigued by the mystery of adult men worship the behinds of women. Adam was our master.

The woman's name was Dina, blonde and beautiful, perfect body, old in her thirties but with delectable legs and behind and, as she ran in the dark, her breasts swayed deliciously. The two sides of the street were in dead silence like never. Everyone in the street stopped talking to listen. The thing lasted at least an hour. When it began, we stopped, half afraid and gathered below a small tree on the street bank and we sat there listening. The entire street listened quietly as though watching a tv show. In some houses we could see people sticking their heads out of the window to hear better. Dina would say "no" but rarely completed the sentences. In the beginning we heard screaming and we stopped. Later we heard slaps, we sat to listen. A boy wanted to go peek in the window, but Adam said no. The man, a so-called Good Joe had a reputation for being angry, if he caught the boy peeking he would crush him. Dina would stay in the house all day, washing clothes, her clothesline was always full, making rice with beans and garlic that Good Joe liked. When she tenderized the steak, we heard the knocking from far. She always sang alone. But Adam had already said, and it had to be true: this whore had a lover. And she really had, otherwise she would be beaten.

Did it stop? Asked a kid and Adam corrected: "wait a bit, it will start again soon". It was a mysterious silence. Adam said she was trying to kiss to calm Good Joe down. The kids thought he was chocking her with his hands, and they made face and eyes of the anguish of the strangled. "None of this, she is on top of him calming him down", said one but Adam said that men don't marry women who are fired up for sex, that is a thing of whores: "it is men who tell her to come on top, dummy". We were always surprised with the things Adam taught us. "Women who are aggressive when naked are whores, they have to do what you tell them or else dump them, they are whores". And someone repeated, "whores" in low voice. I thought she was doing the dishes; I don't know why but if she worked she calmed Good Joe down. "What if she poisoned Good Joe's food tomorrow, I asked and Adam said "Always smell the food before, you dummy. "Women are deceiving things, my uncle detected his food was poisoned one time, he gave such a beating that she took off". It was scary to grow up and marry, you can never drop your guards. Adam might have learned these things from twenty-year-old friends of his. The nights Adam did not come, Rua do Sapo was sad and empty.

Suddenly, everything started again, "whore" and always after this screamed word came the sound of slaps. "Ouch", said someone but Adam was a genius and he explained: "slaps don't hurt, dummy, women like it". How did Adam know so much? Sometimes I saw Adam walking with some twenty-year-olds, grown-ups, they knew a lot, and perhaps taught Adam. Adam knew everything about women and always taught us new things like "they like titty sucking, you dummy". Everyone laughed, what a crazy thing I thought, I'm not going to suck tits". "You have to, you dummy, they go crazy". "You have to hold them tight, dummy". "You have to put your tongue in their ear, dummy". Adam knew all of this, we sat around him, curious, every night. Always when Adam arrived, we ran near him "What's up Adam" and he would soon say something interesting. That night Dina was screaming a lot and Adam always said, "She screams good, come here you whore". We laughed, "you whore", we repeated.

After a while, Dina screamed differently: it seems with pain like hit by a bat, not anymore slaps or belt sounds.

"I think it is a bat", I said but Adam said when it is a bat it hurts less, it hurts more when it is a switch. Dina howled with pain, I knew it was pain because one day she stepped on a nail and screamed the same way. I ran and took out the nail from her foot and she padded my head. I was more than afraid to tell the other kids because Good Joe was crazy, he might kill me. But she screamed so many times that night, quite like in pain, the same from when she screamed that day of the nail. We heard the beating. Good Joe would say "lover", "slut", "fucked", always blowing at the same time, we could not even hear the entire sentences. They said in the city that Good Joe strangled a guy with his own hands, so when Dina screamed then she was not being strangled. We were terrified of strangling like what they did to Tiradentes. "Don't be a dummy, Tiradentes was hanged with a rope". Adam always made us laugh. And Dina howled louder now.

Then, all of a sudden, Dina appeared, quite quickly on the front door and running, passing under a dead tree trunk. Adam said, "what a hottie" and one of the kids in the group said "wow, she is almost naked, she really is a whore". "Shut up dummy, her clothes are torn". Dina was beautiful, blonde, and for the first time a saw her legs, so perfect, her torn clothes showed a bit of her ass, so round that it stood out". She ran in our direction without seeing us, looking like a heroin like on television, with blood running down her face and legs, but running powerfully.

Adam soon started to rub himself, and all of us, from seeing her got hard, while she passed by more slowly. She hid behind the large trunk of a mango tree. I had never seen a woman like that, half naked, bloody, so hot and scared. Adam crouched low where she was behind the mango tree. They said a few things, I don't know what, then we saw her run far, almost to the other block, and Adam came back, with blood on his arm and hand from touching the beautiful Dina. "And?", we asked whispering. "She did not want to fuck", he said and added "She had cuts, I told her to hide at my grandmother's". He was cunning, later he would go see the beautiful Dina. "Wow, she is really hot". "Shut up dummy, Good Joe is outside". The man came out, without a shirt, and walked around the house, he went in, and the candles went out. The silence continued for a few minutes, until one mother after another began to come out, calling the kids "time for bed", "come wash your feet", and we soon began to scatter, thinking of the sounds of that night, and me thinking of cunning Adam, who would certainly try to sleep at his grandmother's house that night to touch Dina. Soon the crowd of kids disappeared, everyone going to sleep on the Rua do Sapo, now calm and silent again. Already in bed, I thought of cunning Adam and the whore Dina, slut, having lovers, deserved the beating. One day I want to be like Adam.

Glass of wine

Of all streets in São Paulo, had I have to walk on Avanhandava? I ran into her. "Hi," she said. We greeted in politenesses, have a coffee? Wine? It was cold. She answered "wine". We walked into Planeta's restaurant at the corner, we sat, we ordered. "How about appetizers? I buy," she said. Her voice was still delicate, soft. She spoke a bit emotional. Despite the years, it is uncomfortable the feeling that I know her well. Her face is still pink, as always, and her blouse very feminine and of good taste. "I buy" I said, without adding anything else.

After so many years her face was still pretty, with the softness of seducing skin. Some wrinkles and tiny lines now show around the eyes. She may be doing botox on the forehead as it was still so smooth. "And you, what have you done all these years?" Always like that, she directs the conversation. Her eyes were still bright as they were on her youth. One gray hair jumped above the black ones. I expected her to talk about politics, about marxism, about the new literature. She still puts on perfume, the same one. She is still delicate when holding the silverware. "Good wine," she said, with the same smile as before. A few people at the place, cold night. "Tell me about you", she asked, with whispered voice. Her hands are still pretty, nicely done nails, a leather ring of good taste. She looked at me with curiosity. If it was not for my wish to run out of there, I would say that she still looked at me with love.

One day we were married. One day we made the first and the last love. One day we exchanged presents, kisses, plans for the future and even spoke of retirement. This meeting should have stayed at a drink of coffee only, I thought. Why did I agree to order wine? This woman has control over me. As we ran into each other, I lost my senses but she immediately knew what to do. "Do you still like orchids?" Why did I ask that? I should have told her I had a meeting. She looked at me with the seme serenity of our first night, of our first year. "Still do", she answered, trying to look me into the eyes but I raised the glass of wine to block, and drank, covering my eyes. "Tell me about these twenty years", she asked. The waiter arrived and saved me with his interruption.

I told her I changed job, I am a technical salesperson now, I did an MBA, studied French, lived near Santa Cruz subway.

"How are you, Tiger? Talk to me" she said, sweetly looking at me with an irritating sweetness. How dare her call me Tiger? A forgotten nickname from so many years. I raised the wine glass to my mouth again "I am fine" and drank as slowly as I could, thinking about talking about another topic. I drank the whole glass, slowly, without moving, without hearing sounds, without removing my mouth from the glass, breaking all the wine drinking etiquettes, hoping time would stretch and she would not be there waiting me drink. The wine now saved me. Slowly I placed the glass on the table and was going to say something about politics. She looked at the table in deep thoughts. She then looked me in the eyes, held my left hand with a grip, her eyes slightly watering. Of so many places that there are in this world, I had to be there, with her holding my hand and looking at me. "Tiger", she whispered. Isn't it a horrible thing to run into someone who still loves us?

Chaw

The man moved to the boarding house, in the room next to me. For being a boarding house, it was luxurious. Each had their own bedroom, there was a small yard, a tree, chairs. The owner was a rude woman but if we paid on time and did not make noise at night, she would not bother us. The man was called Chaw, his nickname for chewing tobacco that came in a fancy little can. From so much chewing, he had horribly black teeth, although perfect in shape. After chewing a lot, he would spit a repulsive black blob in a larger can with a lid that he carried. He moved in with few things: some bags, a suitcase, and some metal and wood objects as he had the habit of collecting things he found on the roads. He was a truck driver, and we were almost the same age, except the beard that he grew long to scare people, perhaps, and also a tattoo on his neck, that gave him the appearance of an ex-prisoner.

Already on the first day he greeted me, putting his four-hundred-pound hand on my shoulder and calling me "my brother". Soon he grabbed his can and made a wad of tobacco, putting it in his mouth between his teeth and the cheek, that gave him a deformed appearance, as though he had a tooth ache. A few hours later he knocked on my door with a can of beer in his hand. The man was insistent, but he certainly was not a scrooge, who might me. We passed the time sitting on the chairs in the yard, close to the little table where he drank beer with much ceremony. He spoke of the truck's shifting gears, that he parked on the empty lot at the side. "The speed determines the gears but, in order to shift you have to rev to synchronize motor and transmission". Annoying dude, what would I care about trucks? But the man found topics to talk about. With time I got used to the dude, who wanted to be my friend despite my being a man of few words.

He had the habit of talking, laughing, and squeezing my knees with his huge fingers, wide and rough. He looked like a friendly giant, but the squeezing was a warning that he could, if he wanted, crush me at any moment. He said he was educated, gone to college, and even taught private science classes. Perhaps it was true, because he spoke very well for a truck driver, not making mistakes for future and past tenses and every once in a while spoke a word that only college professors knew: agnostic, innocuous, conceit. He used words like those, always when he talked about deep topics like divorce or lost friendships, where sentences were not only long but had an air of confessed sadness. With time I noticed that upon saying such sentences he immediately would make a wad of tobacco, put it in his mouth and drink a big gulp of beer: then he would quiet down for a minute, after which he would start an unexpected topic, almost happy.

One day he showed up with a dry root of a tree that he found on the road and brought for me. The root curved strangely, forming the letter P, of my name and he made me hang it in the window. I did it because of his insistence, since he had cleaned to the point it almost shone. And soon we sat for a beer. I sometimes had cheese, that I cut into little squares, and this gave him much happiness, something he showed by squeezing my knee or shoulders. Over months we got used to such routine of cheap leisure, of casual

chats, of beer and laziness in the chairs
in the backyard.

I don't even know why Chaw liked me.
I never had a topic to talk about.
Perhaps it was because I paid attention
to him and asked how, why, when and
allowed him to ramble. There were
other men in the boarding house, but
they were strange, almost all pigs who
threw paper and garbage in the
hallways. But perhaps because I was
the only one who had a college
education and could speak with some
finesse and did not mind him squeezing
my knees and shoulders, which was a
very strange thing were it not a habit.
But in some sense the man was for me
a curious character in the beginning and
so I was all ears.

One time he invited me to go for a spin
in his truck. We left in this monster,
pulling an empty trailer. I soon noticed
that he was a master. He made wide
curves, turned at tight corners and
shifted the thing like he was driving a
car. "How can you drive this good?", I
asked with no intention of praising.
This solidified our friendship. The man
almost stopped the truck, looked in my
eyes and said, "life made me this way,
my brother" and a minute of mutual
sadness followed since that man with

almost a college degree got nostalgic. Soon we were back to the chairs where we drank slowly and let silence fill many seconds till Chaw found the next topic.

Out of the blue he asked me "what you think of the Blacks?". What a shock, we never spoke of others, only us. Divorce, children, childhood friends, lost friendships, or funny things we had seen in life, these were the topics. But now there was Chaw, with a wad of tobacco in his mouth, asking me about the Blacks. "I don't think anything" I answered, fearing the topic. He laughed in his peculiar way, squeezed my knee, and asked me with a tilted head: "Would you marry a black woman?". I thought for a long time, more because I didn't understand this change of topic but also struggling in my head if I would answer the truth or not. But I decided to answer honestly: "no". It was always like this, I thought for too long, which made me come across as not spontaneous, elaborating my answers. He gave me an easy smile, "nor I" and I asked him why. "Because I like to run my fingers through a woman's hair, but with a black woman, the fingers get stuck" and that made us laugh due the surprise of stuck fingers, something I had not thought about. "Drink more buddy". But we stayed quiet for a few minutes, thinking about this thing about Blacks. "My sister married a black stud, now they have three little blacklings, the kids must be grown up now". I said "really?". He answered "really, but she stopped talking to me after I told her about this thing about a white woman marrying blacks, it has been ten years". "Did you know that you can get jail time for that now?", I said, and he stayed quiet and put more tobacco in his mouth. He was always spitting a black blob from chewing. In silence, he spit one on the floor, stepped on it hard, crushing it and said with a laugh "get out of here you black", and we laughed out loud, together, not really knowing why. Then we stayed quiet, in the middle of the night's darkness, as though we were there watching one another.

The sounds of cars and other man in the boarding house was low. It was almost midnight, Chaw leaned against the vinyl cord chair and both of us stayed there, half asleep. He rested calmly like someone who has always been happy. I went inside, got two thin blankets I had got at a paddler's stand, and covered him from neck to legs and sat on the other chair and covered myself, and closed my eyes in the dark, listening to his breathing, almost inaudible despite

the silence. Life is a hard thing to
understand.

Little Party

At around eleven the kitchenette was already full of people, all in their twenties, all already a bit buzzed, wanting sex. The idea was Mario's, who also invited dozens of people our age. We agreed for the lack of anything to do on a Friday night and Alberto offered to buy pinga and Martinis. The three of us shared the kitchenette. It was a place on Nove de Julho Avenue. Just pinga and Martinis, no one had money for appetizers. Some people brought cans of beer, and someone even brought a bottle of wine.

One of Mario's cousins was a stuck-up know-it-all, a student from USP. Without chairs or stools, everyone sat on the floor, and she explained everything about anything. She was pretty and elegant, into hippie stuff. There was a lot of gabbing going on at the same time, small groups of two or three, sitting on the kitchenette's floor, even on the tiny terrace there were people. A record played on a turntable, mainly to muffle the noise so as not to upset the neighbors. The cousin had a tiny waist and a wide, round butt that spread nicely on the wooden floor, attracting the discrete looks of the guys.

In the bathroom, which we painted red, one could hear a couple moaning; by the service elevator another couple made noises; in the living room some kissed. And that cousin spoke of men's primitive brains and the guys sitting next to her on the floor discretely checked out her round butt while she crossed her legs like a hippie, wearing a dress of thin and loose fabric. One looked at me, winked and pointed to her appealing butt. It was past two a.m., several couples rolled on the floor, in the bathroom, on the terrace, but the cousin from USP still spoke, the guys now sitting right close to her slightly touching her legs and soft, round butt.

"Answer me why," she asked, but the guys just laughed, speaking slowly and slurring. One of them hadn't been drinking so he answered: "because it is a macho thing." She wanted to know why men don't turn their back on other men. "What goes on in your mind when there is a man behind you?" she asked the sober guy. The guy was already irritated. The other two got up and left. Other groups of people laid on each other; some, half-naked, had sex right there, several kissed or just stretched out on the ground.

The guy said: "I'll tell you in the bathroom." At this point I was the only observer; she passed by me and entered, completely ignoring me. She walked into the bathroom as though she walked into a classroom. She wanted to learn. The guy walked by me and poked me, "come" and I hesitantly followed him. It is obvious that men do not turn their back on other man, what a stupid girl. But I followed him, jumping over a couple hugging, music playing in the background. The girl from USP liked stupid conversations, she knew no theory, it was all guessing and speculation. In the bathroom I saw the guy with his hands on her waist and she still wanting to learn why men do not turn their back on other men. I stood at the door watching.

The guy told her to turn her back and she did. He lowered her skirt, and she turned suddenly, frightened, "what is this?" she said, and the guy grabbed her by the neck, and she put her left leg on the sink to not fall, showing her thighs and part of her butt, white, delicious, round and seductive. I watched, not knowing if it was a fight or sex, but she was truly hot. Her face was red, and she said nothing, the light was faint, but I could see her closed eyes, her mouth slightly opened like wanting sex. I was going to leave but the guy said, "come in and close the door". I did because I was curious but also because I had no one else to talk to and I wanted to see that hottie from USP up close. Her mouth now opened more; her eyes totally closed seduced even more.

She lowered herself, on purpose or from lack of air, motionless to seduce him even more and he lowered her clothes, exposing her vagina of shaved hairs, smooth and beautiful. And he, right there started to penetrate her and she said nothing in submission. That might be a thing of intellectual women. I watched, with a hard-on, also wanting to have her. Afterall, she was hot, smart and annoying. What a stupid conversation about "why men don't turn their back on other men." The guy moaned in pleasure and got up. She laid there, eyes closed, perhaps tired. He then shut the door and said, "your turn buddy" and I penetrated her hard and firm and she did not even move. She really was delicious. I held her tightly and her body laid there without moving, letting me do whatever I wanted, as though she was sleeping. She might be enjoying being dominated. I got up and she stayed there, with her eyes closed. The guy was ready for a second round again. I left the bathroom, shutting the door after I saw him on top of her again. There they stayed, screwing. I turned out one light and laid among bodies already sleeping or succumbed to exhaustion or sex.

When I woke up, the bathroom couple had left, several other couples had left. The sun rose, annoyingly brightening the kitchenette. I closed the curtain, dressed and left, quietly closing the door. The old man, a neighbor said "good morning" as always as he passed, and I answered the same for we were good neighbors but never talked about a thing. It was a high rise of good, respectable people. It was a memorable party, everyone happy, fulfilled, and wiser on this Saturday that blossomed.

Right Hand

Seu Antonio crossed his legs, put the white hat on the higher knee: "a beer and sausage, please". At night the men met at the square. The tables were for those who ordered beer. The farmhands stoop up. On their feet they learned how to do business, how to manage farms. Soon the beer came, with a chilled glass". The square always got full in the month of February. It was the cotton harvest. The farmhands came at night looking for work, whoever paid the most for the arrouba took the farmhand. But Seu Antonio was known for paying well, for giving pinga and canelinha on Fridays. The farmhands surrounded his table, giving him the turn to talk. It was almost a show.

His word was a contract. Seu Antonio had already hired twenty, needed five more. The son, his helper, whispered to him who was who, who was hard worker and who was a laggard. The crowd had already left, some farmhands still surrounded his table, wanting to know the pay for each arrouba picked. The man straightened his hat, took a gulp of beer and asked: "How many arroubas can you pick?" "Fifteen", answered the man. "Six thirty here at the corner", said Seu Antonio. The son wrote down the name, the man left, happy. They needed one more and there was coming a farmhand, getting close. "That is Maria's John, a laggard", said the son. "Who is Maria?", Seu Antonio asked. "Maria Tanajura, big ass." "Does he drink?" "A little", said the son. The man said "Evening" e soon asked "Do you have work?" "Yes, I do Mr. John," said Seu Antonio. Hired him on the spot. "Seu Antonio, my wife and my daughter pick cotton well, could you hire them as well?" "Yes, the three of you come to the corner at six thirty". The soon looked at his father, frustrated. The wife and the daughter could not pick even ten arroubas. He wrote "John, Maria Tanajura, Daughter". The man left and they raised a beer to cheer. The square was almost empty, the church bells stroke ten at night, in the slow strikes. Time to sleep.

The tractor with an open trailer parked at six thirty in the morning. Seu Antonio opened a coffee thermal bottle and all got excited and surrounded him to drink a hot and sweet morning coffee. Maria Tanajura took two cups, for her and for her daughter from the hands of Seu Antonio, who raised the cups and said "especially hot" and the woman smiled and walked to her daughter, attracting the discrete eyes of everyone. "Good morning Mr. John," "Good morning Seu Antonio," said the farmhand. Soon the tractor left, trailer full of people to the Barra Grande farm for a day of cotton harvest. It was a Friday, it would be the last day of harvest.

At ten in the morning the sun was blazing, the partridges sang their sad sounds far away, cows mooed in the neighboring farm calling their caves and the farmhands sat down under trees, opening their aluminum food containers and drinking water from clay pots, happily thinking of their pays at the end of the day. Mr. John passed a cup of water to Maria Tanajura, who drank and passed it to the daughter. Seu Antonio's son was calibrating the scale. The burlap sacks of cotton were weighed, then inspected. Lazy pickers would urinate in the cotton or add stones to increase the weight. A bunch of criminals, often said Seu Antonio's son. All ate in silence, broken only by fork sounds on the aluminum or by some farmhand asking another farmhand "good?" Seu Antonio had left in his white pick up truck, for lunch.

At around two p.m. the sun was burning. The farmhands, wearing hats, picked the cotton fast, with their fingers bleeding the tiny spikes at the cotton petals. Maria Tanajura and the daughter picked fast, both hoping to reach ten arroubas each. Farmhands who pick more often receive offers for other jobs on the farm, it was always like that. The heat made the hats reflect, from far off one could see vapor trembling above the hats, the partridges sang their sad sounds far away. The son weighed the burlap sacks and dumped everything on a tall pile. He wrote on a little notebook how many kilos. Seu Antonio always had a white hat on, and boots, was sitting on the white tarp cover he installed, from where he would pay the farmhands at the end of the day. From far off, he observed the farmhands. When Maria Tanajura and the daughter finished one bed and turned to start a new one, he waived with his fingers. The son looked at him, the daughter looked at him, a cow mooed far away under the burning sun. It was February.

"Last bed", yelled the son, announcing the end of the day. The farmhands screamed "yay" and all got very excited. A car arrived, bringing pinga and canelinha and Seu Antonio sat at the desk, with a pile of money on his left side, looking at the little notebook where the son had written the kilos, to make the payments.

Each one came with their burlap sacks, weighing for the last time and the son did the math and yelled the arroubas and the kilos to the father. The farmhand would sit on a weak chair by the tarp cover, Seu Antonio calculated, counted the money picked from a pile and paid. "There is caipirinha and pinga" and the farmhand left all happy with the money in his hand. Mr. John came, received his pay and asked if there was work for Monday. "No, Mr. John, the harvest finished". Soon all were sitting on the ground, on top of burlap sacks or standing, drinking a caipirinha or pinga. Maria Tanajura sat down, Seu Antonio calculated, put his left hand on the pile of money, straightened his hat with the right hand, carefully and said "You pick very well, and your daughter too". He calmly and slowly counted the money. "I am adding a bit more for you Ms. Maria," and she smiled. The daughter looked at Seu Antonio's face. "Is there more to pick on Monday?", Maria asked. "No, Ms. Maria," said Seu Antonio. She moved her hand, grabbing the money. Seu Antonio put his hand over her right hand, both stopped, and he said "If you need work, come here tomorrow morning help organize all of this, I'll pay you by the hour". Both looked at each other for a while, without blinking, she looked him in the eyes, he looked her in the eyes, she smiled, the daughter looked at their hands, Seu Antonio's hand on top of the mother's right hand and Maria smiled, looking down, "I will come", and the daughter looked at Seu Antonio and Seu Antonio looked at Maria and Maria Tanajura looked at the table and Mr. John looked at Seu Antonio from far off and Seu Antonio's son looked at the father. Soon, all and also Seu Antonio were happy, drinking canelinha, saying jokes, all men and women smiled and drank and soon they started leaving.

It was a great day. Mr. John picked sixteen arroubas, Maria Tanajura picked fourteen arroubas and the daughter picked eight arroubas. All now had money to go to the circus, to drink guaraná on the square and the three walked home on that Friday, with happy faces, the sun going down. Mr. John went to the bar buy cigarettes and sausage and the wife and daughter went home. There they took a shower, cooked rice and beans and Mr. John arrived, stumbling by the door. The wife Maria Tanajura grabbed from his hands the cigarettes and the sausage and he stumbled to the sofa and the daughter looked at him for a long time and he looked at the daughter with his head low and the mother came and said "let's have dinner, it is all ready" and put her right hand on the father's leg and the daughter looked at her right hand for a long time and all got up, sat by the table and ate quietly.

The Insult

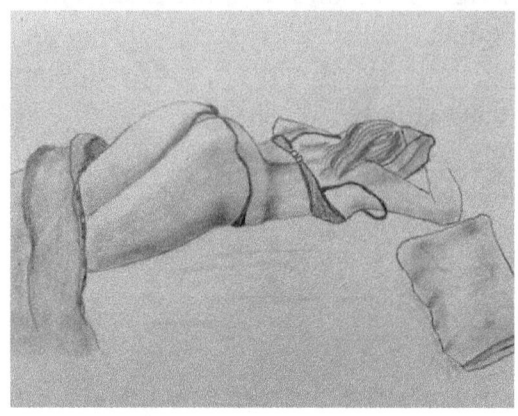

We'd have to refinance the car. "I'll go there Saturday," I'd said. She'd gone out into the kitchen and started cleaning plates, silently finishing the dinner preparations. On Saturday I'd have the courage to ask Fabinho to refinance the car, again. He'd talk to the bank manager and that would be that.

Fabinho owns the dealership. He's an old friend of my wife's and of one of her girlfriends. My wife was still silent, arranging the silverware in a way that made deliberate noise. I had met him by chance in a store, when he'd engaged in a lively conversation with my wife.

When I'd joined them, my wife was quick to introduce us. "This is my husband." Fabinho was quick to hold out his hand. When we needed a car, she'd promptly suggested Fabinho. "You remember him?" When we purchased our second car, we bought it from him too. "I'll talk to Fabinho," she'd said, and the next day the car was in front of our house. So, Saturday I'd go over and ask for the refinancing. How embarrassing.

Friday has come and with it an urge to relax. But Saturday casts a shadow over the dinner about to be served. Dinnertime with the family is sacred. We all have to be there together, talk about cheerful things, laugh, live without haste. Silent, my wife moves between kitchen and table. The kids run around. One yells out the window. Another kicks his sister in the leg. She sobs loudly, desecrating our dinner. She doesn't seem aware of the aura of serenity surrounding our meal. I bellow in irritation, "Everybody go wash your hands for supper!" But the noise goes on, worse, as if no one cared about our sacred dinnertime. Saturday hangs over this meal, refusing to let go of me. One by one I tell them, "Wash your hands – now! Get going." When dad speaks sternly, at least the youngest ones tremble. We sit down at the table, my silent wife serving everyone from her seat.

For half a minute, everyone eats without a sound. My head hangs down, my eyes peer up. I see their pensive faces and my wife with her far-off thoughts. I always tell stories over supper. The kids used to like it when they were younger. Now they strike back. "And then you all ate a ton of candy," strikes back the oldest, who has grown tired of hearing the same old stories. Within instants, their mouths full, they are pummeling each other, knocking over their juice at times. Whenever their mother speaks up, they'll stop and pay attention. They'll quiet down for a minute or two. But this Friday their mother is indifferent.

Before we're through eating, her cell phone rings. She takes an unhurried look at the screen and answers. The kids forget their food, run off, tear about the house. And here I sit, beans in my mouth, still chewing. My wife stands up slowly, sliding sideways off the chair, calling attention to the full curves of her bottom. I watch without lust since the prospect of Saturday's refinancing has once again assaulted my thoughts. I decide not to think about it anymore. I'll go there tomorrow. Everything will be taken care of.

On the phone, someone seems to be talking to her in long sentences, full-page paragraphs maybe. Silent, she replies only "cool," "thank you very much," "that's true," "I agree." She heads into the kitchen, still listening to the voice on the phone, messing with the forks and spoons and every once in a while saying "OK" or "that's true." Our littlest girl suddenly runs in crying, pointing at her older brother, who's running around yelling, defending himself. In the whirling eddy of this commotion, my attention is torn away from the phone call. It seems like the kids are intentionally making a racket. I calm them down, my thoughts now split between them, the phone call, Saturday. "Goodbye," I hear my wife say, her voice more drawn out than usual, a goodbye whose syllables stretch on for a few seconds. Right away the kids rush over to their mother, full of new ideas. They hurry into the living room to do something, and my eyes follow them from room to room, they absorbed in their matters and I in mine.

Night soon falls. In the other room, the kids breathe heavily in their sleep. Fabinho is an old friend of hers. On Saturday he'll get the car refinanced. Lying in bed, my silent wife as if on purpose displays her beautiful legs, which meet the sizeable curve of her buttocks. Her smooth shoulders shine in the half-light. Stretching her legs and her body, she wordlessly announces that she's going to sleep. For a few seconds, my thoughts are pulled into the scene on Saturday, when humiliation awaits me. I can tell she's still awake. "I'll go there tomorrow, don't worry," I say in almost a whisper. She turns over, twisting her perfect curves, and says in almost a half voice, "I forgot. That was Fabinho at dinnertime. He's already taken care of it." "What?" I ask. "I stopped by there this afternoon and talked to him. He's a very nice guy. He took the papers and called to confirm it all."

We're silent in the dark. Her back is to me, her rounded buttocks spreading out softly. She's trying to sleep, silent. I go down to the kitchen, feeling my way in the dark. This Fabinho is an old friend. Disoriented, I think about going back to bed. Her cell phone lies on the table. My heart grows tight in my chest, in a state of confusion. Pressing buttons, I see calls from Fabinho, calls to Fabinho, and other calls all day long. One text message says "Agreed," another simply "Today."

Cell phones are part of the scenes of a family. They invade dinners; they prompt and perpetuate mysteries and secrets. This Fabinho is really one gutsy guy. Awake and adrift, I go back to bed and there she is, sleeping serenely, breathing softly, her nearly naked body an unspoken invitation for sex. Her silence tonight has been an insult, muted words exchanged on the phone, and me watching this silent

body that sleeps as if I weren't here,
perhaps dreaming easily, like an insult.

The Dog

Of all ideas, the most practical one was to sell the dog. They thought about killing him and eating him, but the mother could not do it. It was a good dog. They had sold almost everything: watch, radio, tv, the best jeans, shoes almost new, earrings, a cell phone, a bike, the best cooking pots, and even a leather jacket. The husband, the wife, and the stepson were at the verge of starving. It had been two days since the last meal, they had no neighbor or relatives in town.

They laid down, putting out the candles in the house, since power had been cut off. The dog, also starving, laid down next to the beds with the head between the front paws. The wife asked, "will we find a buyer?" "We will", answered the husband in the darkness of the room, all in the dark, a little house in the back of a vacant house. The dog had been adopted, the boy was from the ex-husband with someone else, maybe it was good to send him away with the ex-husband family. If the dog were sold and the boy sent, it would be easier, she thought.

Almost an hour passed. The husband sat down, in the dark: "I have an idea: we kidnap the clothing store owner, bring him here, demand ransom money, then we get lost". The wife got frightened. Too complicated, they concluded. "We get with him into his house, grab what we can, run off and sell, it is easier", said the wife. "We have ropes, knife, and a gun", said the stepson. "But we don't have bullets", said the mother. "It does not matter", said the husband. The stepson wanted to do it to practice and learn. All agreed. "Tomorrow morning". The dog breathed, sleepy, and all, slowly, breathed with more sleepiness.

In the morning, a light rain fell, messing up the plans. The husband had a simpler idea: Told the wife to stay home, left with the stepson. They would rob the butcher shop. The stepson kept the gun aimed as he was a minor, by law the police cannot imprison him, if he got caught. The butcher trembled, gave whole meat pieces, without bones, the best meats:

rump, sirloin, tri tip steak. All done, in a big bag, they left in a hurry. The stepfather ahead, running. The minor hesitated, the butcher shot him in the head, and he there stayed on the ground. He fell with his head on a piece of meat, he seemed laying on a meat pillow, his blood mixing with that of the meat, running slowly on the curb.

At home the husband fried steaks, telling the wife how it went. "Where is the son?" "He ran to the other side; he will be here soon". The dog got some steaks, swallowing them whole. They seasoned with rock salt left from long time, biting the edges of fat slowly, feeling again the pleasures of the times when they had a job. Proud, she looked at the husband with love and they eat for a while, in silence, relieved, patting the dog's head once in a while.

Brief History of the Kingdom of Oranoslob

this is not fiction.

This story happened in the locale 15.8267, 47.9218, as the bees designated such place after the new emperor's revolution, the king bee Oranoslob, who took over the kingdoms of the east, west, center, north and south after dethroning the queen bee Anavamlid in a bloody war. It was bloody because humans as fascinated with blood. Red thrills and terrorize them. Oranoslob, being a bee, had no blood or heart, as all know e it was as such that Oranoslob became known: the emperor without blood or a heart.

The revolution was so bloody, with so many unknown and also mysterious deaths, that future historians renamed the bee calendar, to have the initial year of 666, in honor of human entities which marked the beginning of Oranoslob's revolution. It is important to remember that the new emperor was the first bee to have an explicit relationship with the humans, where he won many followers. In fact, according to historians, his followers called him God, which is how humans call people with superpowers, and so they crowned Oranoslob as their Otim God, which means god of the good and the evil.

Oranoslob's kingdom was marked by a lot of enthusiasm in the beginning and suffering at the end, for the emperor created his invisible police, which he called the Saicilim. This police was as cruel as the giant bees. The victims were always Oranoslob's enemies and they would be found dead, or most times, they disappeared, just as flowers vanish in the beginning of summer, however, they vanished in the middle of the night, when bees don´t fly. Oranoslob also surrounded himself with aggressive hives, which would destroy any opposition to Oranoslob. His philosophy was that of work, with the motto that "work makes you free". The motto attracted many humans who admired the intense work of bees, although there is historical evidence that the motto had been known in other empires, especially that of Reltih, which vanished long time ago.

Sources close to the life of Oranoslob say that he and his invisible police liked to choke and puncture their victims, or many times to sting them hundreds of times so they would parish in pain for days. Humiliation was also verbal, since Oranoslob mocked of blood which, being red, is not a bee color. Bees have yellow fluid and no blood, though we can certainly say that they, in general, that they love themselves as they work for the common good. But Oranoslob wanted to create his own order, reorganize the world of bees and for such, he counted with the humans who saw in him a kind of new paradigm for life. It was the darkest period in the history of bees. At a certain point, all honey, pollen and propolis, which disinfect the hive finished. Half of all bees perished in starvation and millions of others developed a lethal disease. Oranoslob´s wiseman developed prayers but they charged a lot to enter their temples and so many died without food, with their mouths opened and eyes boggled, and their bodies thinned to bones just as died the humans in the previous Reltih empire. A hungry and bony bee becomes a frightening dryness. In the history of bees there has never been such state of hunger and death.

Oranoslob embodied many human's values. Bees do not have flesh, they have fluids, however Oranoslob gave fluency to many human values, among them the one that bees do not cry. In fact, bees work, they don't cry. But the with the spread of hunger, there was a lot of crying, something hard to detect since to the hungry bees there lacked the energy to cry. So, made a "im im im" sound, this being their last sound before dying. A lot of what Oranoslob said and did was copied by humans who, at the time, had enough science to talk to the bees. Something that humans never learned and Oranoslob could not understand was the fact that from flowers honey is made as from pain heaven is gained, a saying the bees often repeat as reminder that a hive's love overcomes all adversities.

Something Oranoslob never did, however, was to plan and prepare. Out of the blue, giant bees from distant lands appeared. They were bees of giant proportions, of armored bodies, with stingers that do not separate from their bodies like ours, which oblige us to give our lives for a sting. These giant bees decapitated Oranoslob´s followers with a bite, then they ate their bodies or feed them to their babies. Their king was called Sedoreh and the episode became known as the Massacre of the Innocents. The last to be decapitated was the very emperor Oranoslob, but his body was never found and no historical record of the giant bees in the Sedoreh kingdom mention what really happened to Oranoslob. Some suspect that he negotiated his exile and is still alive. His followers created underground groups and to this day they worship their god Otim, who vowed to return. The world of bees will never be the same.

If desired, readers with acute interest
in literature, especially in Minimalism,
or topics related to the general
thematic axis of this book, may
contact the author directly at:

profjohnbarroso@gmail.com